JUST GRANDPA AND ME

BY
MERCER
MAYER

*To Desmond Sansevere
and his Grandpa John G.*

A Random House PICTUREBACK® Book

Random House 🏠 New York

Just Grandpa and Me book, characters, text, and images © 1985 Mercer Mayer. LITTLE CRITTER, MERCER MAYER'S LITTLE CRITTER, and MERCER MAYER'S LITTLE CRITTER and Logo are registered trademarks of Orchard House Licensing Company. All rights reserved. Published in the United States by Random House Children's Books, a division of Random House, Inc., New York. Originally published in 1985 by Golden Books Publishing Company, Inc. PICTUREBACK, RANDOM HOUSE, and the Random House colophon are registered trademarks of Random House, Inc.
www.randomhouse.com/kids
Educators and librarians, for a variety of teaching tools, visit us at
www.randomhouse.com/teachers
Library of Congress Control Number: 84-82600
ISBN-13: 978-0-307-11936-0   ISBN-10: 0-307-11936-X
Printed in the United States of America
22 21
First Random House Edition 2006

My Mom said I need a new suit.

So we went to the city to buy one, just Grandpa and me.

I bought the train tickets,
but I let Grandpa pay.

We went to the big department store.
The revolving door went around and
around and around.

We went around, too,
just Grandpa and me.

I held Grandpa's hand
so he wouldn't get lost.

He did anyway.

Lucky for Grandpa I found him
right away.

We took the escalator to the
suit department.
I told Grandpa to hold on tight
to the rail.

I looked at all the suits
and found just the right one.

Then Grandpa helped me choose
a shirt and tie.

Then we went to the movies.
I sat close to Grandpa
in the scary parts
so he wouldn't be afraid.

We had supper in a Chinese restaurant.
I showed Grandpa how to use chopsticks.

Then we got back on the train.
Grandpa took a nap, but not me.
I couldn't wait for Mom
to see my new suit.

We were so proud—
just Grandpa and me.